Dr. MacTavish's Creature

Story by Chris Bell
Illustrations by Craig Smith

Rigby PM Collection and PM Plus

Emerald Level 25

U.S. Edition © 2006 Harcourt Achieve Inc.
10801 N. MoPac Expressway
Building #3
Austin, TX 78759
www.harcourtachieve.com

Text © 2000 Chris Bell
Illustrations © 2000 Cengage Learning Australia Pty Limited
Originally published in Australia by Cengage Learning Australia

10 11 12 13 14 15 16   1957   13 12 11 10
4500219089

Text: Chris Bell
Illustrations: Craig Smith
Printed in China by 1010 Printing International Ltd

Dr MacTavish's Creature
ISBN 978 0 76 357444 4

Contents

Chapter 1
The New Neighbours

*W*ow. *Look at that!* Alex could hardly believe his eyes. Each item that came out of the moving van was weirder than the last.

Then a huge set of antlers was carried down the ramp. That was it. Alex went across the road to get Brendan.

"Brendan, come and see the weird stuff the new people next door have," he said.

They ran outside in time to see the strangest car they had ever seen. It pulled into the driveway next to Alex's house.

"That must be the new owners' car," hissed Alex.

A very tall man and a woman climbed out of the strange little car. The man waved to the boys.

Before they could wave back, the man began to yell, "No, no, no. Don't carry it like that. Be careful."

The boys looked at the van driver. He was walking down the ramp carrying something odd. The boys' mouths dropped open.

"Do you see what I see?" said Alex.

"I think so," said Brendan. "That is, if you see a ... a skeleton."

The skeleton disappeared inside, followed by the man and woman.

The boys stood and watched the van driver take in the furniture. It was weird, too. There were lamps made from metal. There were odd-shaped chairs, and a table shaped like an elephant.

When the van driver started carrying in boring boxes, Brendan gave up watching and went inside. Maybe it was just an ordinary family after all.

Chapter 2
Strange Howling

Alex stood on his front lawn watching the driver bring a large packing box down the ramp.

The tall man ran out of the house, calling to the driver, "Be careful! That's fragile. Don't hurt it."

The driver looked nervous. He slipped as he stepped off the ramp. A loud groan echoed across the street.

Alex looked up. *What was that?* He expected to see an animal in pain.

But there was nothing there except the van driver, the man, and the box.

It sounded like the noise came from inside the box. What was in there? It couldn't be an animal. There weren't any air holes.

"That man's really weird," Alex told Brendan later. "I think he had some animal trapped in a box."

"Why would he do that?" asked Brendan.

"Maybe it's something dangerous," said Alex. "Something too dangerous to be let out."

"Don't be silly," said Brendan. "Mom said he's a doctor. They're ordinary people, just like us. Their name is MacTavish. They come from Scotland."

That night, a loud wailing noise woke Alex. He lay in bed too scared to move. He listened as a creature howled into the night.

It didn't last very long. But it was a long time before Alex went back to sleep.

"I think Dr. MacTavish really has an animal or some creature trapped over there," Alex said to Brendan the next day. "We've got to do something."

Brendan didn't think so. He looked scared. "What can we do?"

"We're going over there. Tonight, when it's dark. And we're not coming back until we find out what that noise is," said Alex.

Chapter 3

Camping Out

That night, the boys camped out in Alex's backyard.

"What if Dr. MacTavish sees us?" asked Brendan.

"He won't. We'll just look over the back fence. He'll never even know we're there," said Alex.

Brendan didn't look too sure about that. But he nodded bravely.

Alex lay in his sleeping bag thinking about the creature. He hoped they would find out what was making the mysterious noise soon. He didn't have to wait long.

Both boys jumped when the wailing started. It sounded so much closer, outside in the dark.

They crept toward the fence. Slowly they climbed up and peered over the top.

There was Dr. MacTavish standing on the lawn wrestling with a creature. Its long, black arms struggled as Dr. MacTavish fought to hold it. Loud wails howled into the night.

The boys jumped off the fence as they heard the MacTavish's back door squeak open.

They heard Mrs. MacTavish call out, "That's enough for one night. Haven't you tortured that poor thing enough?"

The boys didn't wait to hear any more. They ran back toward Alex's house.

Alex's mother made them a drink and said, "That's funny. It doesn't look like rain. I thought you two didn't care if it rained or not when you camped out."

The boys tried to tell Alex's parents what they had seen.

"There are no monsters or scary creatures around here," said Alex's father. "I think you two had a bad dream. But it is strange you both had the same dream."

"We need proof," said Alex, later that night. "Then they'll believe us."

"How can we get proof?" said Brendan. "I'm not going near that creature or Dr. MacTavish."

"No. We don't have to. We'll use a camera. Tomorrow night, we're going back."

"Oh no," said Brendan.

"Oh yes," said Alex.

Chapter 4

Proof

The next night, the MacTavish's yard was in darkness. Alex put his leg over the top of the fence. "It's too dark. We'll have to go in for a closer look."

"You're joking," said Brendan. "I'm not going in there. No way."

"Come on. No one will see. Mom's gone out and Dad's busy watching television," said Alex.

Brendan shook his head, "It's not your mom and dad I'm worried about." But he followed Alex anyway.

Brendan and Alex tiptoed across the yard. When they were halfway across, the back door squeaked open. They ran and hid behind some bushes.

Dr. MacTavish came out the back door carrying the creature. Its black arms struggled against him.

One black arm shot out, but Dr. MacTavish caught it and pushed it into his mouth. The creature began to howl.

"Quick, take the picture," hissed Brendan.

Alex's hands were shaking. He couldn't hold the camera straight. "I'm trying," he said.

The flash went off.

The creature stopped howling. A loud voice roared into the dark. "You, behind the bushes. Who's there?"

The boys ran for the fence. They could hear Dr. MacTavish coming after them. The creature let out a low groan and fell to the ground with a thud.

Just as they reached the fence, large hands grabbed them from behind.

"I've got you now," said Dr. MacTavish. "What are you two doing?"

Chapter 5

Caught!

"My mom will call the police," yelled Alex, hoping someone would hear.

"Will she now? I think you two had better come with me."

Dr. MacTavish held on to the boys and wouldn't let go. He marched them into his house.

Alex and Brendan looked at the weird furniture and the skeleton and the horned animal on the wall.

"Now we're done for," said Alex.

They both began to get really scared as Dr. MacTavish led them through the house.

"Look what I found in the yard," he called out.

"What are you boys doing here?" asked a voice from the kitchen. And there, sitting at the table with Mrs. MacTavish, was Alex's mom. She didn't look very happy to see them.

As the boys told her what they had seen, Dr. MacTavish began to smile.

"Maybe you should both come outside and meet the creature," he said.

"Go on, boys!" ordered Alex's mom. And they followed Dr. MacTavish outside.

"So you see, it wasn't a creature I was torturing. It was only my poor old bagpipes. I did not mean to scare you both."

Alex and Brendan looked at the bagpipes. They looked at the black mouth pipe. They looked at the bag that groaned. Then they began to laugh.

"I guess it was a bit silly," said Alex, "but it did sound like a creature in pain."

Dr. MacTavish laughed, too. "That's the trouble. And it doesn't matter how much I practice, I never get any better!"